Keena Ford
AND THE SECRET JOURNAL
✶ MIX-UP ✶

MELISSA THOMSON ★ pictures by FRANK MORRISON

DIAL BOOKS FOR YOUNG READERS
an imprint of Penguin Group (USA) Inc.

DIAL BOOKS FOR YOUNG READERS
A division of Penguin Young Readers Group
Published by The Penguin Group
Penguin Group (USA) Inc., 375 Hudson Street,
New York, NY 10014, U.S.A.
Penguin Group (Canada), 90 Eglinton Avenue East, Suite 700, Toronto, Ontario,
Canada M4P 2Y3 (a division of Pearson Penguin Canada Inc.)
Penguin Books Ltd, 80 Strand, London WC2R 0RL, England
Penguin Ireland, 25 St. Stephen's Green, Dublin 2, Ireland
(a division of Penguin Books Ltd)
Penguin Group (Australia), 250 Camberwell Road, Camberwell, Victoria 3124,
Australia (a division of Pearson Australia Group Pty Ltd)
Penguin Books India Pvt Ltd, 11 Community Centre, Panchsheel Park,
New Delhi - 110 017, India
Penguin Group (NZ), 67 Apollo Drive, Rosedale, North Shore 0632,
New Zealand (a division of Pearson New Zealand Ltd)
Penguin Books (South Africa) (Pty) Ltd, 24 Sturdee Avenue, Rosebank,
Johannesburg 2196, South Africa
Penguin Books Ltd, Registered Offices: 80 Strand, London WC2R 0RL, England

Designed by Jasmin Rubero
Text set in Cochin
Printed in the U.S.A.

1 3 5 7 9 10 8 6 4 2

Library of Congress Cataloging-in-Publication Data
Thomson, Melissa, date.
Keena Ford and the secret journal mix-up /
by Melissa Thomson ; pictures by Frank Morrison.
p. cm.
Summary: When she accidentally leaves her journal in Tiffany's apartment,
Keena is afraid that Tiffany will reveal all of her secrets.
ISBN 978-0-8037-3465-4
[1. Diaries—Fiction. 2. Secrets—Fiction. 3. Schools—Fiction. 4. Friendship—Fiction.
5. African Americans—Fiction.] I. Morrison, Frank, date, ill. II. Title.
PZ7.T37195 Kh 2010
[Fic]—dc22
2009044395

For Linda de Castrique and Millie Thomson
—M.T.

To my daughter Nia
—F.M.

AND THE SECRET JOURNAL
★ MIX-UP ★

TUESDAY, NOVEMBER 16
9:30 A.M.

I'm Keena Ford, and this is my notebook. This notebook belongs to ME ONLY. Right now it is writing time in my classroom, and most days during writing time I write in a beautiful journal. On the cover of my journal there are clouds and rainbows and a picture of President

George Washington. But I don't have my journal today, so I am just writing in this plain old notebook.

The reason I don't have my journal is because a very mean person has it and won't give it back. And that person read my journal. And that person is Tiffany Harris, the meanest muffinhead in the whole second grade. Tiffany has been mean for a long time, but the problem of her taking my journal didn't happen until yesterday afternoon.

The problem happened right after I came home from school. I always walk home with Eric and Lamont. Eric is my very best friend, even though we are not in the same class. He is in the second-grade class that is all boys, and I am in the second-grade class that is all girls. And Lamont is a fifth grader. Back when Lamont was a kid, my older brother Brian would make sure he got home safely, so now Lamont has to make sure Eric and I get home safely. Sometimes Lamont used to just walk me to the door of my apartment, but now he ALWAYS has to wait for my mom to open the door before he can leave. The reason why Lamont has to wait is because one time when he left me at the door, I decided to visit my neighbor Mrs. Carlito before going into my apartment. Mrs. Carlito lives by herself, so I wanted to make sure she was not lonely. Also she has a LOT of cookies for someone who lives by herself. When I grow up and live by myself I will have lots of cookies and also some carrots because they help you see at night. Anyway, Mom got pretty mad at me for going to Mrs. Carlito's instead of coming home, so now Lamont has to knock on the door and wait until Mom opens it before he can leave.

Yesterday Lamont had only knocked on the door one time when it flew right open and Mom was already standing there. She had her coat and scarf on.

"Is the heat broken?" I asked.

"No, I am going out," Mom answered. She looked really mad, but I knew she couldn't be mad at me, because I waited with Lamont like I was supposed to. Unless she was mad at me for something I did wrong then forgot about.

"Who are you mad at?" Lamont asked her.

"I'm not mad. Thank you for walking with Keena, Lamont," she said to Lamont in a way that meant Lamont should probably go home now. He ran down the stairs.

"Where are we going?" I asked Mom.

"I'm going to Brian's school," she answered. "And you are going to Tiffany's." She took my hand and started pulling me toward the stairs.

"Oh no I'm not," I said, pulling back. "I will go to Eric's."

"Eric is going to a basketball game with his dad," Mom reminded me.

"Then I will go to Mrs. Carlito's," I explained to Mom.

"Mrs. Carlito is out," Mom said, tugging me toward the stairs again.

"Then I can sit in the car at the middle school," I told her. "I will sit very quietly. I promise."

Mom stared at me without saying anything. I got the feeling that maybe she could be mad at whoever she was mad at already AND be mad at me at the same time. So I stopped tugging and started walking down the stairs with Mom. "Believe me, Keena," Mom said, "I don't like leaving you at the Harrises any more than you like it."

Before Mom knocked on Tiffany's door, she whispered, "Keena, please do not give Sylvia Harris a single reason to say something bad about your behavior. If I get a good report from her, you will be able to watch thirty extra minutes of TV."

"How many shows is that?" I whispered back.

"It's one show," Mom said.

"Hmmm," I said.

"Keena Ford." Mom bent her eyebrows together so that they were almost touching in the middle of her forehead. "Do I look like I want to make a deal with you? Please just behave yourself. It is the right thing to do, and I will be very proud of you. Be a big girl."

"I will be very good, Mommy. I promise," I said. Mom gave me a squeeze and knocked on the door.

Tiffany's mom opened the door. Tiffany was standing right behind her. Right away I could smell roses, because it always smells like roses in Tiffany's apartment. Tiffany's mom burns smelly candles all the time that are supposed to smell good but really they just make you sneeze and wish you could go outside.

"Thanks again, Sylvia," Mom told Mrs. Harris.

"It's no problem, Nikki," Tiffany's mom said. "I just feel awful for you. I hope Brian can fix his behavior before it's too late." She shook her head sadly.

I looked at Mom. I felt worried. I didn't know what Tiffany's mom meant, but she made it sound like something bad was going to happen to Brian.

"Oh, I don't think it's as bad as all that," Mom said to Mrs. Harris. "Brian just needs to learn to stop being a clown at school."

"Oh, I am sure you are right," Mrs. Harris said. She kind of laughed. "Don't mind me. I was just watching this television program about this nice family whose son was in jail. It was the saddest thing. And he first started getting into trouble in middle school. But I'm sure that won't happen with Brian."

"Mmm-hmmm, well, I should be home by five, Sylvia," Mom said. She said it without really opening her mouth, like her top and bottom teeth were stuck together.

"Keena is going to be here for almost

two HOURS?" Tiffany said. She did not sound like she was very excited about having me stay at her house.

"Believe me, my mom doesn't like leaving me here any more than you like it," I told Tiffany. "Right, Mom?" I looked at Mom. She made a laugh sound that also sounded like a coughing sound. Then her face changed colors a little bit.

"Er, I am just sorry to ask for a last-minute favor," Mom said to Mrs. Harris. "So thank you. See you at five," she added, then she kissed me on the top of my head and left me standing there with Mrs. Harris.

"Well, come on in, Keena," Mrs. Harris said. "You poor dear."

At first I had no idea why Mrs. Harris called me "poor dear," but then I decided that she probably did not think it was much fun playing with Tiffany either.

"Ah-choo! Ah-choo! Ah-choo!" I said.

"Oh dear, you have a cold?" Mrs. Harris looked at me like I was poisonous, or a bomb. "Your mom didn't tell me you were sick."

"I'm not sick," I told her. "I think I'm just allergic to your smelly candles."

Mrs. Harris frowned at me. Then she said, "You girls can go to Tiffany's room.

Please do your homework. Then Tiffany must do her workbook pages. Then you can play."

"Ah-choo!" I said again.

Tiffany and I started walking to her room. "Your brother MUST have been very bad if your mom had to go to a meeting at the school," Tiffany said like she knows everything. Tiffany always talks like she knows everything. "I thought you were the only bad kid in your family."

I opened my mouth to call Tiffany a mean name, but then I remembered that I had promised to be very good. So I just said "Mmm-hmm" with my mouth closed, the same way Mom had said it to Mrs.

Harris. Then I didn't talk to Tiffany the whole time we did our homework. I decided that I was not going to say one more word to Tiffany until my mom came back to get me.

My teacher Ms. Campbell just said that writing time is over, so I will have to wait until after school to write the rest of the story of how Tiffany stole my journal because she is mean.

3:30 P.M.

Now it is after school. Here is the rest of what happened at Tiffany's: I finished with my homework and wrote in my journal while I waited for Tiffany to finish her homework and her workbook pages, whatever those are. I started writing that I figured out who Mom was mad at. She was mad at Brian. I did not know why Brian was in so much trouble for being a clown at school. Clowns are funny. I wrote that I didn't like the way Mrs. Harris talked about Brian maybe going to jail when he grew up. It was mean of her to say that, and I have never heard of anyone having to go to jail for being a clown. You might have to go to the circus if you are a clown, but I don't think you have to go to jail. So I wrote that Mrs. Harris doesn't know anything. And then I wrote something very bad. I wrote that Mrs. Harris should just shut up.

A few minutes after I started writing in my journal, Tiffany took her homework paper and left the room. When she came back, her paper had red marks all over it with lots of red writing at the bottom.

"We can't do our homework in pen!" I blurted out. I knew that I had decided not to talk to Tiffany, but this was too important.

Tiffany let a lot of air out of her lungs like grown-ups do when little kids don't understand something. "I'm not turning this paper in," she said like she knows everything. "My mom helped me make the writing better, and now I am going to write it over."

"What is the writing at the bottom?" I asked. I leaned over Tiffany's paper to look at the words in red.

Tiffany snatched the paper away from me. "That's some stuff my mom wants me to add," she said. "So I will write that stuff after I write the rest of it again."

I could not believe what she was saying. "That's COPYING," I said with lots of surprise. "Copying is against the law."

"It's not copying when a mom writes it," Tiffany said. "My mother told me so."

"Are you sure?" I asked her. It still seemed like copying to me.

"YES I'm sure," Tiffany said. "Now you need to be quiet so I can do my work. Or I'm going to tell my mom you think she is breaking the law."

"I did not say that!" I told her. Then I stuck my tongue out at the back of Tiffany's head when she turned around to do her stupid copying.

I took a good look around Tiffany's room. I had not been there since I was in first grade. It still looks almost exactly the same! It is mostly pink and white. And Tiffany always has her teapot and cups all set up.

As I was looking around Tiffany's room, I heard the doorbell, and then I heard Mom's voice. I ran into the hallway to see her. "Thanks again, Sylvia," Mom was saying. Then she saw me. "Oh, THERE you are, Keena," she said. "Get your things, please. And do it quickly."

Mom didn't need to tell me to get my things quickly because I was already running back into Tiffany's room. I grabbed my books off Tiffany's bed and shoved them in my backpack.

When we got back to our apartment, we had a very quiet dinner. I asked Brian about his clown tricks, but before he could answer, Mom said, "I have heard enough about Brian's clowning for today," and told me to eat my peas.

I ate eleven peas. It took a few minutes. I LOVE to eat peas. I love to eat peas one at a time rather than in a big crowded mouthful. While I was eating my peas, I had an idea for how I could help Brian learn to behave better. "Do you know what a fable is?" I asked him.

"Yes, I know what a fable is," Brian

said. His mouth was very full. Brian always puts every single one of his peas in his mouth at once.

"A fable is a story that teaches a lesson," I told him. "In a fable, the lesson is called a moral. Many fables have talking animals instead of people." I know everything about fables because we talked about them yesterday AND today in school.

"You're a talking animal," Brian said in a mean voice. Then Mom made him say sorry.

"Do you know the fable of the city mouse and the country mouse?" I asked Brian.

"Yes," he said.

I told him the fable again anyway in case he couldn't remember all the important parts. It goes like this: Once upon a time there were these two mice. One mouse lived in the city and the other mouse lived out in the country in a field or something. I think the mice were cousins. Anyway, the city mouse went to visit the country mouse, and he thought the country mouse lived a very boring life and ate boring food. So the city mouse said, "Let's go to the city and eat fancy food." And the country mouse said okay. But when they were eating fancy food at the city mouse's apartment, these big dogs came in and chased the mice away. Then the country mouse said, "I am going back to the country, because I would rather eat boring food in a safe place than eat fancy food in a dangerous place." The moral of the story is you should try to be safe even if it seems boring.

I didn't tell the moral to Brian because I wanted to see if he could guess it. "Do you know what the moral is?" I asked him. I smiled at him like my teacher Ms. Campbell smiles at us when she really, really hopes we know the right answer to a question.

"I guess the moral is that I need to

go away from this city," Brian said. He was not even smiling one bit. He looked very unhappy. "It means I should move to the country. I should just move to Maryland with Dad. That's what I want to do anyway."

I felt very shocked when Brian said that. "That's not the moral," I told him. I thought he would have been good at guessing the right moral. What he said was not the moral at all. What he said was terrible. I did not want him to move to Maryland.

"Brian, I need to speak to you in your room," Mom said. Then she said, "Keena, baby, I'll be right back." Mom and Brian walked out of the kitchen. I put a pea on my spoon, but I didn't want to eat it at all. I just set it down on Brian's plate, then I pushed my chair away from the table. I went to my room to write in my journal.

When I got to my room, I looked in my backpack to get my journal. I didn't see it. I tried to remember if I had put it somewhere else when I got home from Tiffany's. I looked beside my bed, under my bed, in my art box, and on my bookshelf. I thought maybe it had gotten squashed down to the bottom of my bag, so I pulled out all my other books. Then I stuck my head all the way into my backpack to make sure it was totally empty. It was! I went into the bathroom to see if my journal was in the bathtub again. It happened once before, and that is a very long story. Anyway, my journal was not in the bathtub. Right then I knew for sure that my journal was missing!

I ran back into the kitchen. Mom was in there. She was washing dishes and talking on the telephone. I don't think she heard me come into the kitchen because she was listening to the phone and the water was whooshing in the sink. I heard her say something about traveling, so I thought she was on the phone with my grandma Haypo. Grandma

Haypo lives in Richmond, Virginia, and we travel a long way in the car to see her sometimes. After a few more minutes, though, I realized she was on the phone with Dad because she said, "Thank you, Curtis." Then she turned around and reached for my dirty plate on the table. She looked toward the door and saw me, and she looked very serious in her face. "Let me call you back in just a minute, Curtis," she said.

Mom put the phone down, then she walked over to me and gave me a hug. When she did that, about a million tears popped right out of my eyes.

"Don't worry about what Brian said.

He didn't mean it," Mom said to me. I told her that yes, I was worried about Brian, but that we would have to talk about it later because for now I was worried about something else. I told her that my journal was at Tiffany's and that I had to get it back right away. "It's an emergency," I said. "She might read it."

"Now, I'm sure it's almost Tiffany's bedtime," Mom said. "And there is no way she will have time to read it tonight. You have written a LOT in that journal." Mom smiled a little bit. "You can just get it from her at school tomorrow," she said, and she gave me a squeeze. Then Mom asked me to get ready for bed and said she would come tuck me in after she talked to Dad again.

Now I am going to watch TV for a while and rest my hand. My hand is tired from writing for such a long time.

TUESDAY, NOVEMBER 16
6 P.M.

Okay, I am ready to write the rest of the story now.

This morning at school I was going to ask Tiffany about my journal right away. But she said something to me first. She came right up to me with a big smile on her face. "You left your journal at my apartment," she told me.

"I know," I said. Then I asked her if I could have my journal back.

"I didn't bring it with me," she said. She was still smiling like crazy. Tiffany never smiles at me unless she is about to tell me something bad. I was pretty sure I knew what bad thing Tiffany was going to tell me.

"You didn't READ my journal, did you?" I asked her. "You better not have read it. That is my private stuff in there."

Tiffany didn't say anything for one minute. Then she said, "Yes, I read it. I read the whole thing."

When Tiffany said that, my face got about a million degrees more hot. I was shocked. I don't know where the water comes from inside you that makes you cry, but it shot up into my eyes in about three seconds.

"That was my PRIVATE STUFF!" I said again.

"Then you should not have left it at my apartment," Tiffany said. She raised and lowered her shoulders very fast like she knows everything.

"I'm telling," I said.

"If you tell on me, I will tell everyone what you wrote in your journal," she

said. "Even the bad stuff. I will tell them all of it."

If Tiffany told all the things I wrote in my journal, I would be in big trouble with a lot of people. Here's some of the bad stuff I wrote: I wrote that Mom's new haircut made her look like an old lady. I had written that Dad was mean for not letting me go to my friend Linny's sleepover on a Saturday just because I stayed home sick on Friday, even after I promised to just lie in my sleeping bag the whole time and rest. I wrote that Linny was a liar because she said she stayed up all night at the sleepover. And I wrote that Eric was getting on my nerves because he was bragging about going to a Washington Wizards basketball game. "Fine, I won't tell," I said.

"And you have to do everything I say," Tiffany told me.

"Like what?" I asked her.

Tiffany did not answer because just then Ms. Campbell asked Tiffany and me why it was taking us so long to unpack our backpacks and did we remember that we were supposed to sit down.

"Sorry, Ms. Campbell. Keena keeps talking to me at the cubbies," Tiffany said.

"I do not!" I said.

"Both of you, please just find your seats," Ms. Campbell said.

Even though I was mad at Tiffany, I was excited for reading time because we were going to read more fables. There is a whole section about fables in our big reading books.

But at reading time, Ms. Campbell told us we did not need to bring our big reading books to the carpet. She said that instead of reading more fables, we were going to read something different. After we all went to the carpet, Ms. Campbell held up a book that said BIPPO AND PECKY on the front cover. There was a drawing of a big gray hippo and a little gray bird with a red beak and a yellow circle around its eye. Ms. Campbell told us to guess what the book was about. I raised my hand high, but Ms. Campbell called on a girl named Shay. "I think Pecky is the bird, and Bippo is the hippo, because Bippo rhymes with hippo," Shay said.

I stretched my hand VERY high so that Ms. Campbell would know I still wanted to say something. She said, "Yes, Keena?"

"I think Bippo is the bird and Pecky is the hippo," I said. "That is more funny than if Bippo is the hippo." Some other people nodded and I heard someone say

yes, that would be more funny. Some-body else shouted that no, it would be better for Bippo to be the hippo. Then a girl named Addy said she thought the hippo was going to eat the bird.

I don't think Ms. Campbell was happy that all those kids forgot to Raise Their Hands Before Speaking, because she made the quiet signal. The quiet signal is when Ms. Campbell puts one hand in the air and one finger over her lips, and then she makes her eyebrows go very close together so that she gets a wrinkle in the middle of her forehead. Ms. Campbell is not a very old lady, but she can make her face wrinkle in lots of different ways to show if she is happy or mad.

When Ms. Campbell made the quiet signal, the rest of us stopped talking and made the signal too. Then Ms. Campbell started reading the story. And we found out that Bippo is the hippo and Pecky is the bird. I was disappointed, but I decided I would try to love the story anyway, and you know what? I did! It was funny. Bippo and Pecky played tricks on a bad zoo guy who was trying to get Bippo sent away.

After Ms. Campbell finished reading the book, she told us she had a special announcement. She said that she read the story to us because someone very important from the story was coming to visit our class on Friday!

"I think it's Bippo!" Addy shouted.

"Bippo's not REAL. It's probably a different hippo," Linny said to Addy. I started getting excited. I had never seen a hippo in real life except for in this game called Hungry Hungry Hippos where you make a plastic hippo's mouth bang up and down so that marbles fly everywhere.

Ms. Campbell made the quiet signal again, then she said that the author of the book was going to visit the second grade on Friday. The author is the guy who wrote the book, and his name is Bob Morgan. Ms. Campbell said we would do some special activities to get ready for Bob Morgan's visit, like thinking up questions to ask him and writing about friendship and stuff like that. People started raising their hands like crazy to say questions they had for Bob Morgan, but Ms. Campbell said it was time for a bathroom break.

I was in front of Tiffany in the line. I used to always try to be in the back of the line, but I don't worry about that kind of stuff anymore because I'm too grown-up for that now. Also I made a famous man fall down some stairs the last time I tried to be in the back of the line. So when we went in the bathroom, I was supposed to go before Tiffany, but she said I had to let her go first.

"That's not fair," my friend Linny said. "Keena was in front of you." I looked at Linny. Then I looked at Tiffany. Linny was being a good friend. I didn't want to make her mad by having Tiffany tell her that I wrote mean stuff about her. So I just said, "It's okay, Tiffany can go first. I don't have to go that bad."

After the bathroom, it was writing time. I wasn't sure what to tell Ms. Campbell about my journal. I wanted to say, "HELP, TIFFANY STOLE MY JOURNAL," but I did not want Tiffany to tell all my secrets. But I also did not want to tell Ms. Campbell that I didn't have my journal, because she would think I didn't take good care of my stuff. So all of a sudden I just told Ms. Campbell that when I was walking to school, a big dog ran into me on the sidewalk and knocked my journal into a puddle and then a bus ran over it. Ms. Campbell raised her eyebrows up high. "Hmmm. You must be very upset," she said. "I know your journal is very important to you."

"Yes, I'm very upset," I told her. That

was true. I was upset because I had just told a whopper to Ms. Campbell. A whopper is a big, big lie. The only part that was true was that I did see a dog on the way to school, but it was pretty small, and a lady was walking it on a leash. Everything else I said to Ms. Campbell was a big fat lie. My lip started wobbling and my eyes got a little wet when I thought about what a big liar I was.

I thought Ms. Campbell might say "There, there," or something like that, but she just gave me this plain old notebook.

"Don't let this one get run over by a bus," she told me.

"I won't. I promise," I said. I felt a little better because I wasn't lying when I promised that.

Mom just came into my room and said that it is time for dinner. After dinner, I am going to ask Mom to go to Tiffany's apartment to get my beautiful journal back! Tiffany will have to give my journal back if Mom asks for it. So good-bye forever, plain old boring notebook!

WEDNESDAY, NOVEMBER 17
10:30 A.M.

Hello stupid old notebook again. We did not go get my journal from Tiffany's after dinner last night because Mom and Brian got into a big disagreement. A big disagreement is some talking in regular voices, then talking a little bit louder, then yelling for about ten seconds, then talking in very quiet voices. I know because Mom and Dad used to have big disagreements before Dad moved to Maryland. Now they just talk to each other in nice voices and say please and thank you in almost every sentence.

Mom and Brian's big disagreement was about basketball. Mom and Dad had decided that Brian was going to have to skip one week of basketball practice and one basketball game because he had been clowning around in class. If Brian was good in class, he would get to play basketball again. If not, he would miss another week. If he missed more than two weeks, then he would have to quit the team.

At dinner, Brian was very mad about his punishment, and he was trying to argue with Mom. He said his teachers were picking on him. He said he could do what he wanted to do in class because it's a free country, which is true because I learned it when I went to the United States Capitol. Mom used her voice that means WATCH OUT, and she said they were not going to discuss it anymore. She said that if Brian wanted to stay on the basketball team he should just do what he was supposed to do and that was that.

So after the big disagreement Mom was kind of grumpy, and she did not want to go to Tiffany's with me. So I went to my room and tried to think up a way to help Brian be good so he could stay on the basketball team. I wanted him to stay on the basketball team for two reasons. First, playing basketball makes Brian happy, and if Brian is happy, then he won't want to move to Maryland. Second, I already made posters for when I cheer for Brian at his basketball games, and if he doesn't get to stay on the team, I won't get to show my posters. One poster says "RARR BRIAN LION" because Brian's team is the Lions, and the other poster says "Keep Tryin' Brian!" I got some little basketball stickers that I put all over the posters.

Thinking about posters and stickers gave me an idea. I decided to make a sticker chart for Brian to help him keep track of how many days he had been good in school. I took a big piece of paper and wrote WAS I GOOD TODAY? at the top. I made five boxes and wrote a day of the week in each box. I did not make a box for Saturday

or Sunday. At the bottom I wrote Good Report = Sticker! Then I wrote Five Stickers = Basketball Team! I taped the sheet with my leftover stickers onto the paper, then I taped the chart to the door of Brian's room.

This morning, the chart was not on Brian's door. Mom said the chart was a very good idea but that she should probably keep the chart so she could put stickers on it when Brian got a good report.

When I got to school today, I told Tiffany that Mom and I were going to come over soon to get my journal. "You better not," she said.

"Why not?" I asked her.

"I don't want to give it back to you yet," she said. "And if you come over with your mom, I will tell her all the bad stuff you wrote."

"You're mean!" I said. "If you tell my mom that I think her new haircut makes her look like an old lady, then that will hurt her feelings. And my mom is always nice to you. Why would you hurt her feelings?"

Tiffany smiled in a mean way again. "I won't hurt her feelings if you do what I say," Tiffany said. "You have to play with me at recess. I want to play Airplane Princess Twins."

"FINE," I said, even though I hate Airplane Princess Twins. I like regular Airplane Twins better. Linny and I made it up. We pretend we are twin sisters on an airplane, and we pretend-fly to different corners of the playground. We pretend the different spots on the playground are famous places where we can do cool stuff. Like we will pretend-fly to Australia and hop around with kangaroos, then we will pretend-fly to the North Pole and visit Santa's Workshop. Airplane Twins is so fun. But Airplane PRINCESS Twins isn't fun at all because you don't get to do any hopping and you don't get to fly to very cold places. You just get to fly to different palaces and castles where you sit inside and drink pretend tea.

Maybe it will be more fun if Linny plays too. Maybe Tiffany will let us play Airplane Princess Triplets instead.

3:30 P.M.

Tiffany would not let us play triplets. She said we were playing twins only. I told Linny I was sorry but that I had promised Tiffany in the morning that I would play with her. Linny looked sad, but she went to play with Shay and Royann on the monkey bars.

Eric came over after school today so we could do our homework in the Homework Hut. It was pretty cold, so Mom gave us some old blankets and towels for the hut. Eric was talking about the visit from Bob Morgan and he was very

excited, but I just kept thinking about Tiffany.

"I am going to ask Bob Morgan if he thinks I should write a book about spies living on a ship," Eric said.

"Tiffany has my journal and she won't give it back," I blurted out.

"Huh?" Eric said.

I reminded him that I had to go to Tiffany's when he was at the Wizards game. I told him that Tiffany read the journal and there was some stuff I had written in there that wasn't too nice. But I said the not-nice stuff was about people in my class. I didn't tell Eric I had written some not-nice stuff about HIM.

"You should go on a mission to get your journal back," Eric said. "You should go to Tiffany's to play, and when she isn't paying attention, you should take your journal back."

"But Tiffany will be mad if I take it," I said. "Then she will be SURE to tell the bad stuff."

"But you can say she is lying," Eric pointed out. "You will have your journal back, so you can say that you never wrote anything bad. Maybe the kids in your class won't believe her."

"Maybe," I said. I was not too sure.

"Hmmm," Eric said. He sat thinking for a few minutes. I let Eric do his thinking. I used to say "Hello!!" when he was thinking for a long time, but now I know that when Eric thinks very slowly, he can come up with a very good idea. I kept working on my math homework while Eric was thinking.

Most of the time when Eric gets a good idea, he'll say "Ta-daaaa!" or something like that. But this time he just let lots of air out of his lungs. I put my math book down. "Do you have an idea?" I asked him.

"I think so," Eric said. He didn't sound very happy. At first I didn't know why, but then when Eric explained the plan to me, I understood why he wasn't excited about it. Eric's idea was that HE would go over to Tiffany's to play, and then he would take my journal when Tiffany wasn't looking. Then Tiffany would be mad at Eric and not at me.

"But you hate playing with Tiffany," I said to Eric.

"But I am going to be a spy when I grow up," Eric pointed out. "Sometimes a spy has to pretend to like doing stuff he hates because it is part of his special mission. Like in lots of spy movies the spy will have to dance with girls because he wants to get secrets from them."

I could not believe that Eric was going to play with Tiffany just to help me fix my problem. He was the nicest kid ever. I felt sad that I had written bad stuff about him in my journal. If I hadn't written the bad stuff in the first place, I wouldn't have to worry about Tiffany telling my secrets.

I told Eric "Thank you" about a million times. I knew he would not read my journal because he takes his missions very seriously, and plus he only likes reading about spies, boats, and what people eat for dinner in other countries. I told Eric that when he was a spy I would try to help him with his missions. Then we pretty much just talked about spy stuff until Eric had to go home.

☆ ☆ 67 ☆ ☆

8:00 P.M.

Tonight was a lot better than last night. Mom told me that Brian got a sticker on his chart, and Mom and Brian did not have a big disagreement at dinner. I decided that it would be okay to ask Brian about something I had been wondering, so I went in his room after dinner. He was sitting on his bed listening to music on his earphones and reading a book for middle school kids called SOMETHING SOMETHING OUTER SPACE. The first two words were too long for me to really read them, but I got the outer space part. His door was open so I had not knocked on it, but I don't think he heard me come in, so I just walked up to him and knocked on his leg.

He jumped about a million feet into the air. Then he shouted, "WHAT?!?" He took one of his earphones out of his ear.

Then I decided maybe it was not such a good idea to ask Brian my question. "Never mind," I said. I started walking to the door again.

Brian told me to wait and said he was sorry he shouted. He said I surprised him. Then he asked what I wanted.

"Um, well, I was wondering if you would show me some of your tricks," I said.

"What are you talking about?" Brian said. He looked confused.

I closed the door so Mom wouldn't hear. "Will you show me some of your clown tricks? That you do in class? I won't tell Mom," I said.

Brian looked confused for another second, but then he rolled his eyes at me. He took out his other earphone. "When my teachers say I'm being a clown, it doesn't mean like a clown at the circus. They are just saying they think I should be quiet and sit still all day long. And when I try to talk to my friends or joke around, they tell Mom I'm breaking the rules," Brian said.

"Oh," I said. I felt my shoulders go down a little bit. I was disappointed.

"Any more questions?" Brian asked me.

I looked around his room for a second. "Um, can I sit in your beanbag chair?" I asked him.

Brian asked if I would be quiet so he could read, and I said yes, so he said yes, I could sit in his beanbag chair. I walked over to the other side of his bed and sat in the squashy chair under the window.

Brian picked up his book again, but he

didn't put his earphones back in. I decided I would ask him one more question.

"Brian?" I said.

He said "What?" again, but a little bit nicer.

"Why do you like to be a clown at school?"

Brian said that he didn't really like to be a clown, he just didn't like people always making him do stuff he didn't think he should have to do. I nodded my head a LOT when he said that. "I know that's right!" I said. I don't like people making me do stuff I don't want to do either. Especially people like Tiffany Harris.

"Now are you going to be quiet?" Brian asked me. I nodded, and he started reading again. I sat and watched. It was pretty boring to watch somebody read a book, but I felt safe sitting all smooshed down in Brian's beanbag chair.

After a lot of quiet, boring minutes, someone knocked on Brian's door and opened the door at the same time. I couldn't see over the bed, but I knew it was Mom because she always opens the door at the same time as knocking, and plus she is the only other person who lives in our apartment. She said in a kind of worried voice, "Do you know where your sister is?" and Brian pointed at me in the beanbag chair. Mom walked around the bed so she could see me.

"Sorry, Mommy. I will go back to my room now," I said. I started to get up, but it was kind of hard because I was smooshed down in the beans very well.

Mom looked at me and then at Brian. Then she said I could stay in Brian's room for a little while! Then she left.

I was excited that I was getting to hang out with Brian, but pretty soon it got boring again because he was just reading, reading, reading. After I got really bored, I thanked Brian for letting me sit in his chair, and then I went back to my room to write in my note-book. My notebook isn't so super-bad to write in, but I will be happy when I get my journal back tomorrow after Eric's special mission.

THURSDAY, NOVEMBER 18
10:30 A.M.

I really hope I feel happy after Eric's special mission, because right now I don't feel happy at all. Today we got our jobs for when Bob Morgan from BIPPO AND PECKY comes to visit. My job is to say a little speech about friendship. Ms. Campbell said I can talk about why some of my friends are important to me.

I would have liked my job of making a speech except it has caused two problems. The first problem is that Tiffany said I have to write my friendship speech about HER or she will tell the bad stuff in my journal. The second problem is that I think Linny is feeling sad that I'm playing with Tiffany all the time now and not playing with Linny, because she told me she wishes that we could play together sometimes. Then she said that if her job was writing a speech, she would write about me because she thinks I am a very fun friend and she thinks we have fun playing games like Foursquare and Airplane Twins. So now I don't know what to do for my speech. If I don't write it about Tiffany, she will tell everybody all my private stuff and Linny might not be friends with me anymore. If I do write about Tiffany, then Linny still might not be friends with me anymore, because she might think I am friends with Tiffany only. And I'm not friends with Tiffany. Not even for one second!

Linny's job for the visit is to go get Bob Morgan from the school office and walk down the hall with him until he gets to our classroom. Tiffany's job is to ask some of the questions we all said. That's not a good job for Tiffany, because she does not really like to ask questions. She just likes to boss people around all the time.

3:30 P.M.

Eric is doing his special mission right now! I really, really hope he can get my journal back.

5:30 P.M.

Eric got my journal back!!!!!!!!!!!!!!!!!

He didn't give it to me yet, though. That is part of the plan. Tiffany is not supposed to know that Eric is giving the journal back to me. There are these video cameras in our building that make sure no robbers come in or that people don't litter. Eric said if the cameras see him bringing the journal to me, Tiffany might find out. So instead Eric called me when he got back from Tiffany's.

"Mission accomplished!" he shouted, and then he just hung up.

I called him right back to ask him how he got my journal.

"At first I was just looking around Tiffany's room, but I didn't see your journal anywhere. So I thought maybe she hid it somewhere," he said. He was breathing really loud, like he had done a million jumping jacks. "So I told her I wanted to play hide-and-seek. But Tiffany said no. She said we had to play Princess Rescue."

"Oh no," I said.

"It was kind of like hide-and-seek, except Tiffany was the princess who had been captured by the bad zoo guy, and she wanted me to be the prince who saved her," Eric told me.

"Yuck," I said.

"So I said no, I would only play if I could be Spider-Man. And she said okay. So I went out of the room and she hid in the closet. And I knew she was in there because she was making crying princess sounds. But I didn't rescue her. I just looked everywhere else in her room for your journal. But it wasn't anywhere!" Eric was still breathing really loud.

"So then did you rescue her?" I asked him.

"No," he said. "She just kept crying louder and louder and then she yelled I AM A BEAUTIFUL PRINCESS TRAPPED IN A ZOO YOU BETTER RESCUE ME RIGHT NOW ERIC, and then her mom came in and asked what was going on. And then she rescued Tiffany even though she wasn't part of the game. And she said if I could not behave, then I would have to go home. And she gave Tiffany some extra math to do. Then it got really boring."

"So when did you get my journal?" I asked. I started to wish that I had not asked Eric how he got my journal. He was taking a very long time to explain it.

"So then I went to the bathroom, and when I came out, I saw there was a big bookshelf in Mrs. Harris's room. So I just went in her room," he said.

"Oh no," I said. I could not believe it. Eric never did dangerous stuff like that!

"I saw that your journal was on the tippy-top shelf," Eric said. "So I climbed

up the bookshelf like Spider-Man. Then I put the journal under my shirt. And as soon as I went back in Tiffany's room I told her I had to go home because I felt very sick and I was afraid I was going to throw up all over her bed."

"Good one," I told him.

"So like I said, mission accomplished!" Eric shouted. And I said good job. Then we hung up.

I will never write anything bad about Eric in my journal ever again. He was so nice to get my journal back. The only problem now is that I won't be able to write in my journal at school because then Tiffany will know that Eric gave the journal back to me, and plus Ms. Campbell thinks my journal is gone forever.

8:30 P.M.

Since I didn't have my journal tonight, I was going to sit in bed and write my speech, but I was having a hard time getting comfortable. I tried to think of a more comfortable place to sit and write, and I decided that it would be more comfortable to sit in Brian's beanbag chair again. When I went to his room, he said, "Oh boy, it's you again." Then he said, "What, are you going to start coming in here every night?"

"Okay!" I said. I was happy that he invited me to start visiting every night. I walked right over to the beanbag chair and sat down.

"What's that notebook?" Brian wanted to know.

"It's my journal for right now," I told him. "I had some problems with my other one."

"I like that notebook much better," Brian said. "It doesn't look so girly."

When Brian says stuff like that, most of the time I stick my tongue out at him. But I thought if I stuck my tongue out, he might ask me to leave his room. Instead, I asked him if he had gotten a good behavior report that day.

Brian rolled his eyes, but then he said

yes. And he said, "It's kind of annoying that you want to check up on my behavior all the time, but I guess you are just trying to be a good kid."

Then all of a sudden I just started crying. "I'm not a good kid," I told Brian. "I'm a bad kid." I told him I wrote all kinds of bad stuff in my journal. I even wrote bad stuff about my very best friend.

Brian laughed at me. I told him it was not nice to laugh at a crying little sister, and he said, "It doesn't make you a bad kid just because you wrote some stuff in your journal that wasn't nice. You can write what you want in your journal."

"But everybody might find out the bad stuff I wrote," I said. I told him all about Tiffany, and how Eric got my journal back but that Tiffany still knew all the bad stuff I wrote. I told him about Bippo and Pecky and how I had to give a speech in front of the whole second grade. I said that Linny would be sad if I wrote my speech about how great Tiffany is. But Tiffany said I HAD to write about her.

"So what, you're going to let Tiffany boss you around for the rest of your life?" Brian asked.

"I don't know," I told him. "I guess so. Maybe I should move to Maryland too.

But I would miss Mommy. But if you move to Maryland and I stay here, I will miss you," I said, and I started to cry again.

"I'm not moving to Maryland, dummy," Brian said. "Dad has to travel too much for work, and there would be no one to stay with me. I just said that because I was mad."

"Oh," I said. I felt about a million times better in about two seconds.

"Plus I have to stay here to make sure you don't do dumb stuff like let Tiffany Harris boss you around," Brian said. "Just let her say what she wants to say and don't worry about it. That's pretty sad that she thinks she has to force people to play with her. Even though she's mean, it's sad no one likes her."

"I guess," I said. "But I would like her if she would just be nice! I can't like her if she is mean all the time! And I can't like her if she just wants to play princesses all the time and won't let anyone else pick the games. And I can't like her if she tells all my private stuff. If she tells what I wrote, all my friends will be mad at me."

"Even if she tells what you wrote, your friends won't be mad for very long," Brian told me. "Your friends are pretty cool. And plus, little kids don't have very good memories."

"We do too!" I said. I can remember almost every time someone has made me mad since kindergarten. I can't really remember from preschool, though. "Do you really think my friends are cool?" I said with lots of surprise.

"Yeah, they're okay," Brian said. I couldn't believe it!

"Am I cool?" I wanted to know.

"You're cool if you don't let Tiffany Harris tell you what to do," Brian said. "Just say whatever you want to say in your speech, and if she tries to tell you what to do, just say, 'It's a free country.'"

"It's a free country," I said. "That's

true." Then Brian asked me if I would be quiet so he could read. I turned to the back of my notebook and started writing my speech.

FRIDAY, NOVEMBER 19
3:30 P.M.

TODAY WAS THE GREATEST DAY OF MY LIFE. I met a famous writer, people clapped for my speech, and I found out Tiffany Harris is a LIAR. And Mom let me drink two cups of punch even though it is loaded with sugar.

First, I met a famous writer! Bob

Morgan! He has written TEN books. Five books are about Bippo and Pecky. He answered lots of questions from the second-grade kids. And he even answered some questions from the parents! Mom was there with her video camera, but she didn't ask any questions. I wrote down Bob Morgan's answers to the questions in the back of my notebook so I wouldn't forget what he said.

Next, I gave my speech! Five kids gave speeches, but mine was the longest. I got a little nervous about making a speech in front of kids and grown-ups and a famous guy. But I gave my speech in a loud voice anyway because

I would NOT have been cool if I had gotten scared and run away or something. I did not look at Tiffany for my whole speech because I knew she was not going to like it.

My speech was about how I am very lucky to have three best friends. I said I have a best friend in my class named Linny, a best friend in my building named Eric, and a best friend in my family named Brian. Then after I talked about my three best friends, I told a fable that I made up. It was about Bippo and Pecky, but I also made up this other hippo at the zoo named Skippo. I named him Skippo because I know Bob

Morgan really likes hippo names that rhyme, and I wanted him to like my fable. So anyway, Skippo is mean to the other hippos and Bippo tries to teach him to be nice. After I said the moral of my fable, I said THE END. People started clapping, so I bowed. Then Ms. Campbell told me good job and I could take my seat now.

After all the speeches we had a little party with fruit punch and cake. Addy's mom made the cake, and Addy used icing to make Bippo and Pecky on the cake. Then at the bottom she wrote THANK YOU, BOB MORGAN, but she ran out of space, so the THANK YOU part was extra big, BOB was a little smaller, and MORGAN was all jammed up so you couldn't really read it. But I told Addy it looked really good because I know it is hard writing on cakes.

I was having a really fun time at the party because lots of people were telling me they thought my speech was very, very good. And Linny gave me a hug and said I was nice. She said she liked the part of my speech where I said that even though Linny and I have disagreements sometimes, it's okay because we are still very good friends.

I was standing beside Linny and eating my cake when Tiffany came over to me. She looked mad. She said, "I'm going to tell Linny what you wrote about her in your journal."

"What are you talking about?" Linny asked Tiffany.

"Keena wrote something mean about you in her journal," Tiffany said.

I felt very brave after I gave my speech and Linny said that yes, even though we had disagreements, we were still friends. "I don't care what you say," I told Tiffany. "It's a free country. You can say everything you read in my journal. I don't even care."

"You READ Keena's journal?" Linny sounded very shocked.

I decided to just tell Linny what I wrote before Tiffany could tell her. "I wrote that I didn't believe you stayed up all night at your sleepover," I said. "I think I wrote it because I was very sad that my dad didn't let me go to the sleepover. I'm sorry."

Linny moved her shoulders up and down in the same way that Tiffany does to act like she knows everything. Except when Linny did it I didn't mind, because I knew it meant that she wasn't mad at me. I felt about two million times better in one second.

Just then Tiffany's mom walked over and said she thought I was a good little speaker and that I should always remember to stand up nice and straight when giving a speech.

"Tiffany read Keena's journal!" Linny said to Mrs. Harris. "You should tell her not to read someone's private stuff."

Mrs. Harris looked surprised that Linny said that to her. "Tiffany certainly did not," she said. "I took that diary away from Tiffany as soon as I saw that Keena left it, because Tiffany needed to do her extra workbook pages. Tiffany is learning to do third-grade math." Then Mrs. Harris turned to me. "I'm not sure where I put your diary, but I'll try to remember to look for it."

"That's okay," I said. "I got a new one."

Mrs. Harris walked away to go talk to Ms. Campbell. I looked at Tiffany. She didn't look too happy. "You lied!" Linny said to her.

"I played Airplane Princess Twins for no reason!" I said. "Why did you lie?"

Tiffany said she didn't know, and she moved her shoulders up and down.

"It's not nice to lie," Linny told her. Then she asked Tiffany if third-grade math was hard. Tiffany said it wasn't that hard but that she didn't like it. Then she just talked to us normally for a few minutes. She didn't say she was sorry about lying, but she didn't say anything else mean. So after Tiffany left, Linny and I decided that we will ask Tiffany to play with us at recess next week as long as we can play just regular games and not the princess kind.

SATURDAY, NOVEMBER 20
11 A.M.

I am at Dad's. I decided to just go ahead and finish writing in this plain old notebook since I'm almost done with it. This morning when Dad came to pick up Brian and me, Mom showed Dad Brian's chart that had three stickers on it already. Dad said, "Wow, what a beautiful chart! Did you buy that from a professional chart maker? It must have been very expensive." And I told Dad that I was the one who made the chart! Brian only has to get two more stickers. I think he can do it, but if not, I will make him another chart for the next week.

Before we left with Dad, Mom made everyone watch the video of my speech. Mom, Brian, and I sat on the couch, and Dad sat in this old rocking chair from Grandma Haypo's. When I started talking about Brian, all of a sudden you could hear this sniffing sound on the video. But you could still hear me talking because I talked loud. Then when the video was

over, Brian said my speech was pretty good! Dad said he thought I was fantastic. Everyone asked me questions about the part of my speech that was about Eric. Mom said the sniffing sound was from her crying because she was proud of Brian and me for being nice people even if Brian was trying to make her crazy with all his clowning. Then Brian said Mom's crying sounded like a horse breathing. And Mom said Brian better watch out.

FRIENDSHIP
A Speech by Keena Ford
Dedicated to Bob Morgan

Hello, my name is Keena Ford. I am going to give you a speech that has two parts. The first part is about my three best friends. The second part is going to be a fable.

I have three best friends. One of my best friends is named Eric. Eric lives in my building, and he goes to this school. Except he is in the boy class. Eric and I have been best friends since we were four years old. Eric and I do a lot of projects. One of our projects was making a Homework Hut out of a big refrigerator box. When I have a problem, Eric tries to help me fix it. He helped me a few weeks ago when I cut off my hair by accident. We tried to make a yarn braid to go where my real braid used to go. And this week he helped me with another problem. The way we fixed the problem might have been against the law, so I won't say what it was, but I will just say thank you, Eric.

My next best friend is Linny. Linny is in my class. I like Linny because we play fun games together. I also like her because now that we're in second grade she doesn't get mad about little stuff anymore. If someone tries to make her mad, she just says, "So what?" and "Whatever," and stuff like that. I like Linny because we can have disagreements but then we can still be friends.

My other best friend is my big brother, Brian. He is the best big brother in the whole world. He lets me come in his room when he's not busy, and he talks to me about my problems. Sometimes he says mean stuff to tease me, but when I feel sad he tries to make me feel better.

I am so happy that I have a big brother, and I am happy he is not moving to Maryland. He has a beanbag chair.

Now it's time for the fable. This fable is called SKIPPO IS NOT NICE TO BIPPO AND PECKY.

Once upon a time two best friends named Bippo and Pecky were at the zoo. They are the same Bippo and Pecky from Bob Morgan's book, so I hope it's okay that I used them for my fable. Anyway, Bippo was mad because this mean hippo named Skippo knew a secret about Bippo. And Skippo said he would tell Bippo's secret to EVERYBODY if Bippo didn't do everything Skippo said. Skippo wanted Bippo to play with him all the time instead of playing with Pecky. Then Pecky got sad. So Bippo told Skippo, "You are not the boss of me." Skippo started to tell Bippo's secret, but Bippo sat on him so that no one could hear what Skippo had to say. And you didn't know this at the beginning, but Bippo was a lot bigger than Skippo and that's why he could sit on him.

The moral of the fable is that if you want to be someone's friend you should just be nice.

Now you learned a lesson and you

learned about my three best friends.
I love you, Bob.

THE END

Answers about Bob Morgan

47 years old

Virginia

Ten books

Two kids

Stay in school

Yellow

Too hard to decide

Mint Chocolate Chip

Next year

Yes

DON'T MISS KEENA'S OTHER ADVENTURES!